While Their Parents Were Sleeping...

WRITTEN BY PATTI PAVOLKO

ILLUSTRATED BY ABBY PAVOLKO

To order additional copies of this book, contact:
Xlibris
844-714-8691
www.Xlibris.com
Orders@Xlibris.com

Library of Congress Control Number: 2022915117
ISBN: Softcover   978-1-6698-4267-5
         Hardcover   978-1-6698-4268-2
         EBook   978-1-6698-4269-9

Print information available on the last page

Rev. date: 12/09/2022

Contents

Kinley and Grammy's Saying

I will never leave you,

I will always take care of you,

And I will love you forever and ever . . .

No matter what.

Acknowledgments

I would like to thank my wonderful husband for supporting me throughout this project. Thank you to my daughter, Leslie, for helping me submit this book. Also, thank you, Abby—my daughter-in-law—for her beautiful illustrations and for making my book come alive. To my best friend, Tonya; without you, I never would have had the confidence to work past the first chapter. Thank you. And lastly, thank you to Kinley who was the inspiration for this book and who also helped Mommy color some of the pictures.

The Wood Sprites

Once there was a little girl whose name was Kinley. She was beautiful, intelligent, and caring. She had dark wavy hair that flowed down her back. Her eyes were huge and the color of milk chocolate. Her Grammy loved her with all her heart.

Whenever Kinley was sad or upset, Grammy would say,

"I will never leave you,

I will always take care of you,

And I will love you forever and ever . . .

No matter what."

Like Grammy, Kinley did not like to go to bed. She had too much to do, books to read, crafts to make, and she did not want to miss a single adventure. What if she missed something exciting while she was asleep?

At night, Mommy would help Kinley get ready for bed. She would go potty, brush her teeth with cinnamon-flavored toothpaste, and put on her favorite purple unicorn pajamas. Kinley and Mommy would say their prayers, remembering to ask God to bless Mommy, Daddy, and Kinley's brother and sister, Wesson and Haylen. Then Mommy would sing "Twinkle, Twinkle Little Star" and "Baa, Baa, Black Sheep" to Kinley.

As soon as Mommy would leave the room, Kinley would get out of bed. She would look at some books, play with her stuffed animals (her horses were her favorites), and build a safari tent with the many quilts Grammy had made her.

Now Daddy would come in.

He was six feet tall and had lots of muscles. He could pick
Kinley up with one enormous hand. His eyes
twinkled whenever he looked at his little girls.
His beard was three colors—brown, red, and
white. His eyes twinkled when he talked to her.
Kinley thought Daddy could do anything.

Daddy would say,

Kinley, Mommy needs to go to sleep.

Daddy needs to go to sleep.

Go to sleep, Kinley!

One day, Kinley and Grammy were in Grammy's greenhouse planting seeds when Kinley let out a big yawn. Grammy asked Kinley if she was tired.

Kinley answered, "No, I'm not tired. I hate going to sleep!"

Grammy agreed! "I understand completely!" said Grammy. "I never want to go to bed either.

There is always a sewing project or some craft I want to work on. Sleeping seems like such a waste of time. When you go to bed, repeat our saying, close your eyes, and wait for an adventure to begin in your dreams. Sleeping will not be a waste of time, it will be fun."

That night Mommy said prayers and sang with Kinley. Daddy came in and gave her a hug and a kiss. He said, "Please, Kinley, go to sleep."

Kinley thought of Grammy and said,

"I will never leave you.

I will always take care of you.

And I will love you forever and ever, No matter what."

Then she closed her eyes and waited for her adventure to begin.

Pretty soon, Grammy pulled up outside with her bright blue four-wheeler. "Come on, Kinley, want to go on an adventure?" she asked.

"Yeah!" Kinley yelled, as she climbed up in front of Grammy. She held on to the handlebars and pretended she was driving. Grammy put the four-wheeler in gear and pressed on the gas. Away they went!

Grammy and Kinley drove down a narrow, mowed path. On their left was a tall cornfield swaying in the breeze. To their right stood a field of tall pine trees. They crossed a driveway and went down a small, steep hill. They swerved to the right and climbed up, up another hill. Next, they flew over a dirt bridge with water flowing under it. Along they went, passing between two enormous tulip trees. They swerved to the left, and Grammy yelled "Duck!" as they went under some extremely low branches. They continued and splashed through a huge mud puddle. "Splishy, splashy!" they yelled.

Next, there was a very steep, muddy hill.

"Hold on," said Grammy. Down the hill they went. They heard the mud squishing under the big four-wheeler tires. Up another hill and over another bridge, at last, they were at an opening to a soybean field.

Grammy's House

Corn Field

Creek

Gaswell Road

Gas well Road

Forest Bridge

Soybea Field

Great Big Mud Puddle

Another Bridge

Creek

Four Wheeler

Grammy asked, "Left or right?"

"Right," yelled Kinley. They started down the path.

Soon Grammy slowed the four-wheeler down. In the bright beam of the headlights, they saw two little men. They were wood sprites!

The wood sprites were little elves who lived in the woods. They were dressed in camo, from their hats to their boots. Kinley asked, "Who are you?"

"I am Bob," said the shorter one.

"I am Bill," said the one with the red beard.

"Come hunting with us," the little men invited.

Grammy and Kinley slowly followed the wood sprites until they stopped under a tall hemlock tree. There was a ladder going up the side of the tree that led to Daddy's tree stand.

"What are you doing under my Daddy's tree stand?" Kinley demanded.

"We left our jars here," answered Bob. He pulled out two mason jars with holes punched in the lids.

"Lightning bugs," answered Bill. "We use them to light our way as we travel through the woods."

"What fun!" said Grammy, "I used to catch

lightning bugs when I was a little girl." She shut off the four-wheeler, and the four

hunters—Bob, Bill, Kinley, and Grammy—searched for and captured jars full of flickering

lightning bugs.

When each jar was filled with twenty bugs, Bob said, "Our job is done. Please take this

jar as a thank-you for your help."

"Thank you so much," said Kinley, as she accepted the jar.

Kinley and Grammy climbed back on the four-wheeler. "Goodbye, Bob. Goodbye, Bill. Thanks again," Kinley called to the little men.

"Goodbye!" yelled the wood sprites. "Please come visit again soon."

Grammy drove Kinley back home. Kinley held the jar of fireflies to light their way along the path.

When they reached Kinley's house, Grammy took Kinley back upstairs and kissed her good night.

"Good night, Grammy. I love you," Kinley said sleepily.

"I love you too," said Grammy.

Soon, Kinley heard the four-wheeler start up and Grammy driving off. Kinley fell fast asleep.

When Kinley woke up the next morning, she had a big surprise. At the end of her bed was a quart jar full of lightning bugs! Mommy wanted to know where the lightning bugs came from.

Kinley smiled. "I wonder," Kinley said.

Mommy looked at Kinley with a funny look on her face and just shook her head.

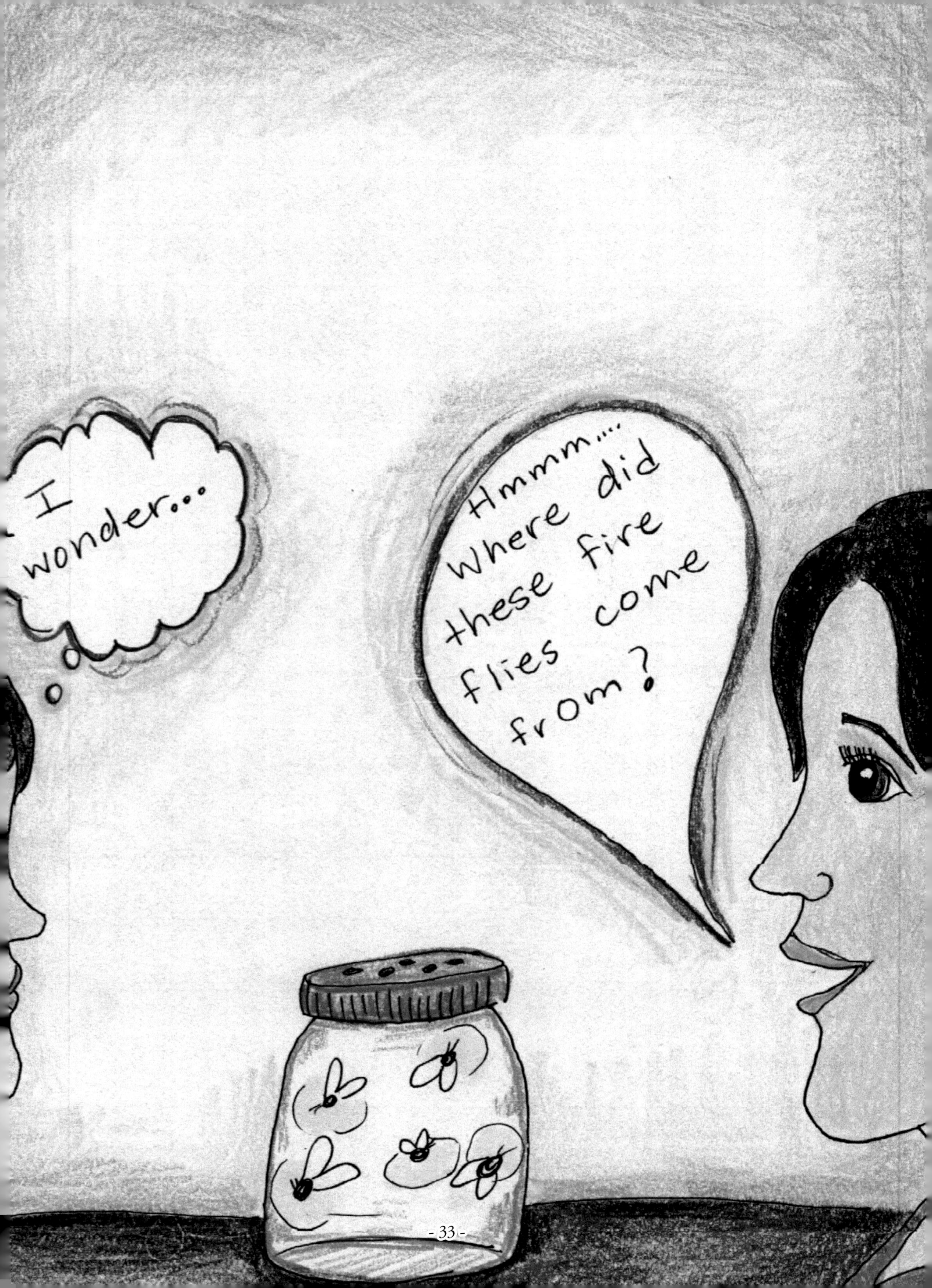
I wonder...
Hmmm.... Where did these fire flies come from?

As Kinley ate her breakfast, she wondered what her next adventure would be. Now she could not wait for bedtime to find out.

Black Beary Bear

Kinley loved her first adventure with Grammy. She wondered if it really happened. Maybe it did; after all, there was that jar of lightning bugs by her bed in the morning.

At bedtime the next night, Mommy helped Kinley get ready for bed. She brushed her teeth with her electric toothbrush, and she put on her wild mustang pajamas. Mommy and Kinley said their prayers, and Mommy sang "Twinkle, Twinkle Little Star" and "Baa, Baa Black Sheep." Mommy said, "Good night, honey. I love you. You went to bed like a big girl last night, I hope you do the same tonight."

Daddy came in and hugged and kissed Kinley goodnight. "Hey, Sweet Pea, you sure went to bed like a big girl last night. I was very proud of you!"

"I love you, Daddy," said Kinley.

"I love my Sweet Pea," said Daddy.

Kinley wanted to make Mommy and Daddy proud of her again, but it was more exciting to see if the adventure was real. When Daddy left, Kinley thought of Grammy's saying and said to herself,

"I will never leave you,

I will always take care of you,

And I will love you forever and ever . . .

No matter what."

Kinley closed her eyes and hoped she would go on another adventure tonight. She loved meeting the wood sprites, Bob and Bill, and she had fun catching lightning bugs with them.

After a while, Grammy came into Kinley's bedroom. "Ready for another adventure?" Grammy whispered.

"Sure, Grammy. Can Wesson and Haylen come with us?"

Wesson is Kinley's older brother, and Haylen is her younger sister.

"Of course," said Grammy.

Kinley went across the hall to Wesson's door. "Hey, Wesson, are you awake?" asked Kinley.

"What's going on?" Wesson asked.

"Want to go on an adventure with Grammy and me?"

"Yeah," Wesson answered while rubbing his eyes and searching for his glasses.

When they turned to meet Grammy in the hallway, their baby sister Haylen was there.

"Where goin'?" she asked.

"We are going on an adventure, and you can come with us," said Kinley to Haylen. "But you will have to put some clothes on if you want to come along."

Haylen was two years old, and she didn't like to wear clothes. She always went around the house in her Minnie Mouse diaper. "Okay," said Haylen, as she went back into her room. When she came out, she had on a pair of blue jeans and a sweatshirt. As usual, the sweatshirt was on backward.

"Everybody ready?" Grammy asked.

The three children whispered, "Yes!"

"Good thing I brought the utility vehicle tonight. We all would not have fit on the four-wheeler. Kinley, you sit in the middle. Wesson, you hold on to Haylen."

As they pulled away, Grammy checked to make sure her pails were in the back. (She had a special adventure in store for this night.)

They drove around the soybean field and past Daddy's tree stand. Kinley noticed there was a mason jar resting against the tree. Was that the wood sprites?

Next, they drove through an opening in the trees that led into the woods. They followed the path Daddy had made ten years ago. They went down a steep hill and crossed over a bridge and around a muddy curve. Along they went until they came to another opening. They turned left and there was a clearing.

They parked the UTV in front of some tall bushes full of plump juicy berries.

"Grammy, are we going to pick blackberries?" exclaimed Kinley.

"Bereez?" asked Haylen.

"Yes!" yelled Wesson. "Are you going to make a blackberry pie?"

"Yes, yes, and yes to all of you," laughed Grammy. "Haylen, can you count the pails in the back?" asked Grammy.

Haylen counted, "One . . . two . . . three . . . four."

"Good job. One for each of us," said Grammy. Grammy handed out a bucket to everyone. "Let's get to work," she told them. "Stay close, and, Haylen, you need to stay by me."

Everyone started searching for the plumpest, juiciest berries they could find.

They were picking berries for a little while when suddenly there was a low rumble. Kinley asked, "What was that?"

Wesson said, "Did you hear that?"

Haylen said, "Grr!"

Grammy listened and there it was again, louder this time. "Everybody, slowly move behind me," Grammy instructed.

Wesson stepped back into something mushy. He said, "Is that bear poop?"

"Poop, poop," said Haylen.

"Yuck!" yelled Kinley, as she backed away, holding her nose.

"Shh," whispered Grammy.

Suddenly, they looked up and out of the bushes walked a very tall, three-hundred-pound black bear!

"Grr, grr, grr," roared the bear.

The children huddled behind Grammy. Grammy looked straight at the bear. "You just stop it right now!" she yelled. "This is our woods, and these are our blackberries! Back off, bear!"

The bear started to cry.

"Aw, poor bear," Kinley said, "What's your name?"

"I, I don't have one," said the bear.

"A talking bear?" questioned Wesson.

"Boo-hoo," said Haylen.

"I just moved to these woods because I could not find any food near my last home. I'm so hungry, my tummy is growling."

"Here, you can have this bucket of berries," said Grammy, feeling bad for the way she talked to the bear.

"Let's name you Black Beary Bear," suggested Kinley.

"I like that name," said the bear.

"Good. Your name is now Black Beary," announced Wesson.

"What else do bears like to eat besides berries?" Kinley asked.

"Honey?" asked Wesson.

Haylen said, "Sweet."

Black Beary said, "I love honey."

"So, let's do this." Grammy had an idea. "We will find you a beehive. All the honey will be yours, and all the blackberries will be ours. What do you think?" she asked Black Beary.

"I think that's a great idea," exclaimed the bear.

"Great," said Grammy. "Let's load up in the UTV, Black Beary, I think you'll fit in the back."

They rode along, searching for a beehive. Deep into the woods they drove, looking to the left and to the right up in the tall trees. Soon, Kinley pointed and said, "There's a beehive up in that oak tree."

"Look, there's more than one," said Grammy. "Count them, Haylen."

"One, two, three," counted Haylen.

"Great," Grammy said enthusiastically. "Go try some of the honey, Black Beary."

He swiftly climbed up the tall oak to the first gray beehive. He dipped his enormous paw in the hive. When he pulled it out, it was dripping with thick, sweet golden honey. He licked his paw and tasted the yummy honey. "Yum," cried Black Beary, as he dipped his paw in for some more of the tasty treat.

"All right," said Grammy, "How's that?"

"Great! My tummy says thank you. Thank you," said Black Beary between licks of thick honey.

"So let's get back to our berry picking," said Grammy.

"Can I help?" asked Black Beary with a hungry look on his face.

"No," Grammy laughed. "I think we can handle it ourselves. You need to start collecting your honey," she said.

"Oh, yes, my honey," Black Beary smiled.

"Load up, guys," she called to the children.

"Goodbye, Black Beary! Hope to see you out here again sometime," called Grammy over the motor of the UTV.

The children waved to Black Beary, and Kinley asked, "Did anybody else notice that Black Beary didn't ask us if we wanted to taste the honey?"

They all laughed as they drove back to the berry patch. They filled their pails with plump, juicy blackberries. All except for Haylen, that is. She put more in her mouth than in her pail. Grammy noticed she stuffed some berries in her pockets; she hoped they didn't stain her shirt. They put their pails in the back of the UTV and headed home.

"I had so much fun," Kinley told Grammy.

"I liked meeting Black Beary and naming him," added Wesson.

"Love berries," laughed Haylen with a mouth full of berries and juice running down her chin.

When they got home, Grammy tucked each one of them into bed and kissed them good night. "I love you, guys," she told them.

In the morning, the children woke up and went down to breakfast. They found Mommy and Daddy at the dining room table with a puzzled look on their faces. Daddy asked, "Anybody know where this pail of blackberries came from?"

Kinley looked at Haylen and Wesson. "I don't know," answered Kinley.

They all giggled, and Wesson asked, "What's for breakfast?"

"Blackberry pancakes?" asked Haylen.

Felicity Frog

Kinley wasn't sure which adventure she liked the best. Meeting the wood sprites and catching lightning bugs were great fun. But so was meeting and naming Black Beary Bear. The berries were tasty and real; these adventures had to be real. She had proof. She hoped Grammy would make a blackberry pie to share with them. She was happy to have Haylen and Wesson with them on their last adventure.

The next night, prayers were said, songs were sung, and Kinley kissed Mommy and Daddy good night.

I will never leave you,

I will always take care of you,

And I will love you forever and ever . . .

No matter what.

It wasn't long until Grammy entered her room.

"Are we going on an adventure?" asked Kinley.

"Of course," answered Grammy. "Are Haylen and Wesson coming?" asked Grammy.

"You bet we are," said Wesson.

"Goin' venture," chimed Haylen.

They all got into their seats in the UTV. Grammy started driving down the path past Daddy's tree stand and the blackberry bushes. She stopped at a small puddle and told the children to wait in the UTV. She walked over to the puddle and looked at it.

"Yes, this will do. Come over here, guys," she called to the children.

Wesson helped the girls out of the UTV. "What are we doing here?" asked Wesson.

"Is our adventure a mud puddle?" asked Kinley incredulously.

Haylen asked, "Play mud?"

Grammy laughed and explained that, yes, their adventure was indeed going to take place at the mud puddle. "See those little black things swimming in the puddle?" asked Grammy. "They have little tails."

"I see them, they are very small," said Wesson.

Kinley said, "They are funny looking."

"Bugs!" cried Haylen.

"No, they are not bugs, Haylen, they are tadpoles. When I was a little girl, we called them pollywogs. There was a creek near our house. I would take one of my mother's quart jars and catch them. My dad would punch a hole in the lid so I could watch them grow. That's what I want us to do so that you can watch the tadpoles grow into . . ."

"What?" asked Wesson.

"Grammy, what do the tadpoles grow into?" Kinley asked anxiously.

"Bug?" Haylen sighed.

"No, they turn into frogs."

"What!" Wesson exclaimed.

"You are kidding, right?" Kinley asked.

"How?" asked Haylen.

"Through a process called metamorphosis," answered Grammy.

Wesson questioned, "Meta-mor-pho-sis?"

Kinley tried, "Meta-moosis?"

"Moo," Haylen laughed.

"So I brought along some quart jars for each of you to catch some tadpoles. Here they are," she said. "Count them, Haylen."

"One, two, three," counted Haylen.

Grammy said, "Good job, Haylen. Now just dip your jar into the water, let some water flow in, and take the jar out. Then you could check to see if you caught anything."

Suddenly, the water splashed all over Grammy's face. "What the heck," cried Grammy. "Where did that come from?"

One step closer and I'll...!!!
Who is that?
Who do you think you are?
Don't talk to my grammy like that!
Gooey mud! YAY!

"I can tell you where it came from," cried a small voice, "it came from me!"

"Who is that?" asked Wesson.

"What a tiny voice," said Kinley.

Haylen asked, "Who?"

"Who's there?" asked Grammy.

"It is I. I am on the big rock, and my name is Felicity Frog."

"Why did you splash my grammy?" asked Kinley.

"What do you think you are doing?" Felicity asked.

"Well, I was going to have the children catch some tadpoles so they could watch them turn into frogs. There are quite a lot of them here," answered Grammy.

Felicity asked, "Did you happen to think that those tadpoles came from someone's eggs? Mine?"

"Oh my goodness," cried Grammy. "I never thought of that. I am so sorry, Felicity, please accept my apology."

"Well, okay," said Felicity.

Grammy asked, "Do you think the children could take a few home to watch them change into frogs?"

"Could we, please?" asked Wesson.

"We'll take real good care of them," pleaded Kinley.

"One, two, three?" asked Haylen.

Felicity replied, "Well, you know, this puddle is pretty small for all my children and friends."

"Mm," Grammy thought, "how can we help you?"

"The excavator," Wesson answered. "Dad's excavator would work."

"Yes," Kinley said, "that's a great idea, Wes." She continued, "Dad could dig you a small pond for all your children and friends."

"Ride xvater," cried Haylen happily.

"Great idea," said Grammy. "Wesson, you and Haylen go get your dad. He was in his workshop when we left. Make sure he lets Haylen ride in the xvater," Grammy laughed.

Grammy and Kinley talked to Felicity, while Wesson and Haylen went to get their dad.

They rushed to the house, hoping he was still in the workshop. When they entered the workshop, Dad said, "What in the world are you two up to?"

"Xvater," replied Haylen.

Wesson did his best to explain to Dad what was going on. Finally, Dad said, "Okay, I give. I'll go start the excavator up."

Wesson handed Haylen up to Dad.

"You lead the way, Wesson," instructed Dad.

When Kinley saw them coming, she jumped up and down, waving her arms for Daddy to see her. When they got to the puddle, Daddy shut down the machine and helped Haylen out.

"So, what are you up to this time, Mom?" he asked.

"Well, I wanted the children to watch some tadpoles turn into frogs, but I never thought I would be taking someone's children," Grammy said in a rush. "I'm sorry. This is Felicity Frog. Felicity, this is my son."

"Nice to meet you," said Daddy.

"I'm happy to meet you too," said Felicity.

"So, as I was telling you, this puddle is way too small for Felicity's family and friends. The children thought maybe you could dig her a small pond."

"Please," all three children pleaded.

Felicity said, "If you could do this for me, I would let your children borrow some of my tadpoles."

So Daddy talked to Felicity about how big and what shape she wanted her pond to be. Then he climbed up into the excavator.

"My turn to ride," said Kinley.

"Climb on up, sweet pea," Daddy laughed.

Daddy worked the knobs and turned and moved the excavator. In no time, he had dug a little pond for Felicity.

HAYLEN
WESZON KIMLEY DAD

GRAMNA

"Oh!" she exclaimed, "this is even better than I had hoped for. Thank you ever so much."

"No problem," Daddy said. "I hope you are happy here."

"Come, children, you may each take three tadpoles home with you," said Felicity. "But will you bring them back after you have watched them grow, please?"

"You bet," the children answered.

Daddy helped Haylen.

"Count them, Haylen," said Grammy.

Haylen counted, "One, two, three."

"Perfect," said Daddy.

Grammy helped Kinley, and Wesson caught his own tadpoles.

"Thank you so much," Grammy said to Felicity.

"Of course," said Felicity, "and thank you for our pond. Please take good care of my children."

"We will," replied the children.

"Okay, who's riding back with me?" Daddy asked.

"It is my turn," said Wesson.

"That's right. Haylen and I will ride back with Grammy," said Kinley.

They waved goodbye to Felicity and said they would see her soon.

Back at the house, Daddy shook his head at Grammy and said, "I don't even want to ask you what is going on."

"Good," said Grammy, "I'll put the children to bed." She tucked each one into bed and told them she loved them. They thanked her for another wonderful adventure.

The next morning at breakfast, Mommy asked, "Does anybody know where the jar of tadpoles came from?"

The children looked at Daddy with grins on their faces.

Daddy had a sheepish grin on his face as he said, "Gee, I don't know."

Sparkling
Gemstone Forest

"Lightning bugs, blackberries, and now tadpoles," Kinley thought. She had lots of proof; her adventures must be real.

"Good night, Mommy. Good night, Daddy. I love you very, very much," said Kinley. Mommy said, "We love you, too, Kinley."

"We are super proud of you, Sweet Pea," Daddy continued. "You have been going to bed like a really big girl. Keep it up."

Mommy and Daddy left Kinley's bedroom.

Kinley hoped there would be another adventure tonight. She had so much fun with Grammy, Wesson, and Haylen. She repeated their saying,

"I will never leave you.

I will always take care of you,

And I will love you forever and ever…

No matter what."

"Hello, Kinley, are you ready to go?" asked Grammy.

Kinley exclaimed, "Grammy, I thought you'd never get here! I'll get Haylen and Wes."

Wesson and Haylen were already in the hallway. Wes had his glasses, and Haylen was struggling with her sweatshirt.

"Here, let me help you, Haylen," said Kinley. "Go?" asked Haylen.

"Yes," Grammy said. "Let's go."

They loaded up in the UTV in their usual spots. Away they went through the children's backyard and around the corn field, past Daddy's tree stand, and by the blackberry patch. Black Beary waved as they went by.

They continued past Felicity's Pond, and saw Felicity and her friends swimming and basking in the moonlight. Felicity asked about her tadpoles, and the children assured her they were all doing fine and well on their way to becoming healthy frogs.

Kinley asked Grammy about tonight's adventure. Grammy said she didn't have anything planned. She thought they would just drive around and see what they could find.

Grammy drove on through the woods for a short while when they spotted what looked like a long dark tunnel. "What do you think, guys?" Grammy asked.

Wesson said, "Let's go for it!"

Kinley said, "Yes, I want to see what is at the end of the tunnel."

Haylen said, "Go!"

They slowly entered the dark tunnel. Once they were inside, they noticed various colored gemstones on the walls. They glittered red, white, pink, green, and blue.

"How pretty," Kinley sighed.

When they left the tunnel, they passed under a brightly colored rainbow: red, orange, yellow, green, blue, and purple. They looked around and everything seemed extra bright and pretty. The sun glittered and sparkled. The leaves on the trees were an extra bright green.

A beautiful fairy flew up to them. She was dressed in a lovely shade of red. "My name is Ruby," she said, smiling. "Welcome to Sparkling Gemstone Forest."

"Hello," Grammy said, "I'm Grammy, and these are my grandchildren Haylen, Wesson, and Kinley."

"Nice to meet you," smiled Ruby. "If you are hungry, feel free to visit our kitchen where Opal will make you anything you ask for."

Another fairy dressed all in white smiled at them. "The unicorns are to your right. Feel free to try to ride them, but there is a secret to being able to ride." Again, she smiled.

When they looked to the right, they saw beautiful white unicorns grazing in a pasture closed in by a wooden fence. Each unicorn's white coat shimmered with either blue, red, pink, green, or blue sparkles.

"They are so beautiful!" Kinley said in awe.

"Bootiful," said Haylen.

Of course, their horns shimmered with gold.

"I want to go see the unicorns," said Kinley.

"Yes," said Haylen.

"Let's eat," said Wesson.

"Two to one," Kinley announced. "Let's go see the unicorns!"

"Ucorns," said Haylen.

"Okay," said Wesson reluctantly.

"Before you leave," instructed Ruby, "take a hike along the Sparkling Gemstone Path. You may each choose one gemstone to take home with you as a souvenir."

"Wow!" said Grammy.

They headed right to the unicorns. Kinley was so excited she couldn't hold still.

Another fairy dressed all in green was named Emerald. She explained to the children that they could pick a unicorn to try to ride. "However," she paused, "not everyone can ride a unicorn. There is a secret to being able to ride."

The children wondered what the secret was. Wesson attempted to ride a unicorn that shimmered with silver glitter. Her name was Diamond. As soon as Wesson got his foot into the stirrup, Diamond took off and Wesson hit the ground.

"Are you alright?" Grammy asked Wesson.

"Yeah," said Wesson grumpily, as he dusted off his behind.

Kinley carefully put her foot in the stirrup and pulled herself up onto a gorgeous blue unicorn named Sapphire.

"Hi," Kinley said. "My name is Kinley."

"I'm Sapphire," the unicorn replied, as she started walking around the pasture.

Kinley was thrilled. "Thank you for letting me ride you, Sapphire," she breathed.

"Thank you for believing in me," said Sapphire. "That is the secret to riding a unicorn, believing."

"Can my sister ride with me?" asked Kinley.

"You know the rule," answered Sapphire.

"Oh, she believes," promised Kinley.

Grammy picked up Haylen and put her in front of Kinley. The girls rode Sapphire around the pasture for forever, according to Wesson.

When Wesson proclaimed for the fifth time that he was hungry, Grammy helped the girls off Sapphire.

"Thank you, Sapphire," Kinley said, "Bye." "Come again," replied Sapphire.

They went on to Opal's kitchen. Wesson had his favorite, spaghetti and meatballs. He quietly told Grammy it wasn't as good as hers, and she beamed. Kinley had a refreshing chocolate milkshake, and Haylen asked for strawberry ello, which was Jell-O.

When they were finished, they walked the Sparkling Gemstone Path which led around the unicorns' pasture. Glittering gemstones littered the path with beautiful shades of purple, blue, pink, red, green, and silver. Wesson choose a ruby gemstone because red was his favorite color. Of course, Kinley picked an amethyst because purple was her favorite color. Haylen chose a diamond because it is her birthstone. Grammy liked that idea and chose a blue aquamarine, her birthstone.

When they were back at the tunnel, they got into the UTV. They said goodbye to Ruby, Opal, Emerald, and Sapphire.

"Thank you for the delicious spaghetti and the ruby," said Wesson.

Kinley said, "Thank you for the unicorn ride and the amethyst. I had a wonderful time."

Haylen said, "'Thank you."

They waved, as Grammy headed the UTV under the rainbow and through the tunnel.
Now they were back in their woods and on the path home. When they got home, Haylen
was asleep in Wesson's lap. Grammy carried her into the house. She took the children to
their rooms and kissed them good night. Wesson and Kinley hugged her and thanked her
for the great adventure they had. Haylen still was fast asleep.

The next morning the children went downstairs. They were eating breakfast when Daddy came in from the barn. Mommy asked, "Where in the world did these beautiful gemstones come from?"

The children smiled and said, "I don't know."

George and Duncan, the Squirrels

The next night Kinley said,

"I will never leave you,

I will always take care of you,

And I will love you forever and ever . . .

No matter what."

Kinley thought about the Sparkling Gemstone Forest. It was hard to believe it really happened, but she had the gemstones to prove it.

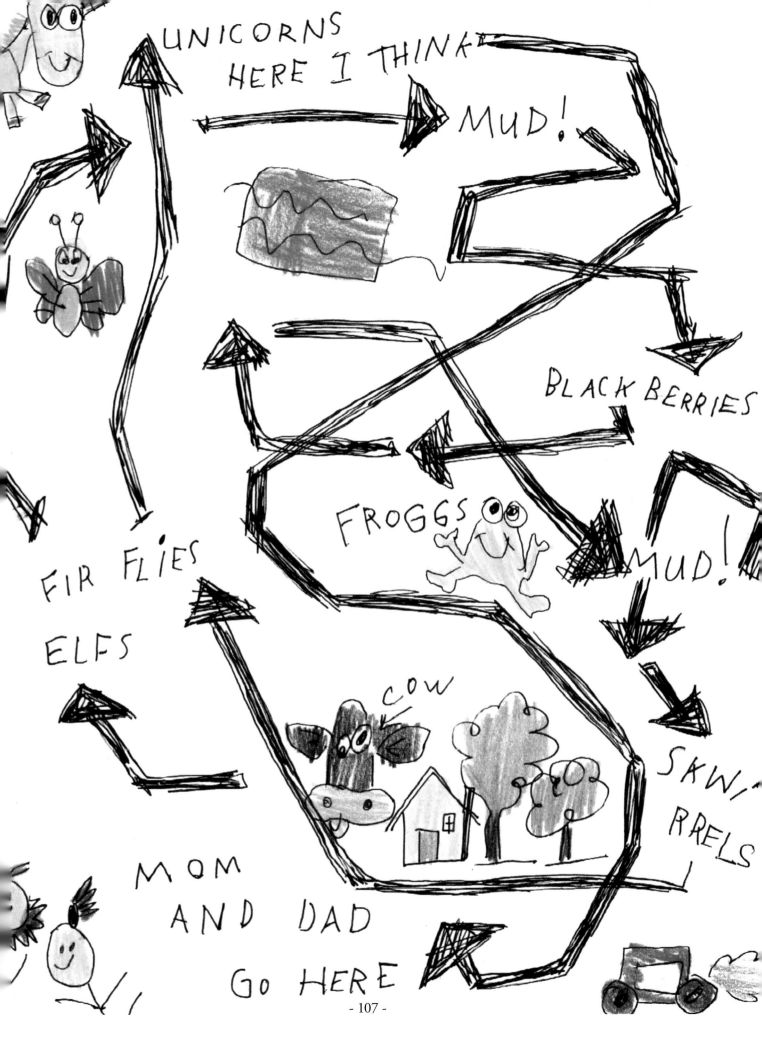

Wesson and Haylen walked in, and Wesson said, "We're ready. Where's Grammy?"

Haylen said, "Ready." Her sweatshirt was on right!

Grammy walked in and said, "Wow!" You are all ready, so let's go."

"What are we doing tonight?" asked Wesson, as he buckled the seatbelt around Haylen and himself.

"We are going to gather black walnuts for a yummy recipe I have for apple walnut bread," answered Grammy.

"Are you going to share with us?" asked Wesson.

Grammy said, "If we find enough walnuts, I'll make two loaves, one for Papa and one for you."

"Yes!" yelled Wesson.

"Yummy!" whispered Kinley.

"Taste?" asked Haylen.

Grammy was laughing as they headed down the path. The wood sprites were by Daddy's tree stand and everyone waved. Black Beary Bear was dining at his beehive. He waved as he enjoyed his honey. When they passed the tunnel that led to the Sparkling Gemstone Forest, Kinley wondered how Sapphire was doing.

Finally, Grammy found some black walnut trees. She parked the UTV and told the children they could get out. They all got out, as Grammy took four baskets out of the back. She found a walnut and showed it to the children. "This is what we are looking for," she said.

"How do you eat this?" asked Wesson.

Grammy explained how they must use a nutcracker to break open the shell to get to the nut inside.

"Oh," said Wesson.

"Oh, nuts," said Haylen, and everyone laughed. They started looking for walnuts, staying close to each other.

"Ouch!" yelled Wesson, rubbing his head. "I just got hit with a nut!"

"It probably fell from a tree," Grammy said.

"Hey, that hurt," cried Kinley. "I just got hit with a stick."

"Ouchy!" cried Haylen, and showed Grammy an acorn.

As Grammy stepped toward Haylen, she felt something striking her legs. When she looked down, there was not one but two gray squirrels beating at her legs with sticks.

"Hey!" exclaimed Grammy. "What are you doing?"

"Yes," demanded a small voice. "What are you doing!"

"We are picking walnuts for a yummy recipe Grammy has for apple walnut bread," explained Kinley.

"These are our walnuts, and we are gathering them for winter," explained one of the squirrels.

"Well," said Grammy, "technically, this is our woods, so the walnuts are ours."

"Well, we live in these woods and we have to have food to eat over the winter," answered one of the squirrels.

"I'm George, and this is Duncan," he said.

Grammy said, "Happy to meet you. I'm Grammy, and these are my grandchildren—Kinley, Haylen, and Wesson. What do you think of this idea? Will you share the walnuts with us if we promise to only take what we need for our bread and leave the rest of the walnuts for you? Then we will help you gather your nuts. You can climb the tree, and we will hand the nuts up to you."

"On one condition," answered George.

"What's that?" asked Grammy.

Duncan replied, "Will you sing a song and dance for us? Gathering nuts is so boring."

"You got it," said Kinley. She went over to Haylen and Wesson, and they whispered for a little while. When they finished, Haylen and Wesson began singing "Twinkle, Twinkle, Little Star." As they sang, Kinley danced a beautiful dance she learned in her ballet classes. She leaped and twirled and looked as if she were floating. George and Duncan had smiles on their faces as they swayed to the music.

When they finished, Grammy and the children helped the squirrels gather a big pile of walnuts. Then the squirrels climbed the tree, and Grammy and the children handed walnuts up to them. When their work was done, They gathered *just enough walnuts to make two loaves Of bread. They thanked George and Duncan for sharing, and the little squirrels thanked them for their help and for singing and dancing for them.*

"Please come see us again," said Duncan.

"We'll be back," said Grammy, as Wesson loaded their baskets of walnuts in the back of the UTV. They got settled into their seats and drove away.

They drove along the path through the woods to the children's backyard. Once again, Grammy parked and saw that Haylen had fallen asleep again tonight. She took the children up to bed and kissed them good night. They said goodnight sleepily.

The next morning, Mommy said, "There is Apple Walnut Bread for breakfast." "Did you get this at the store?" she asked Daddy.

"Uh, no," replied Daddy.

She looked at the children.

"We don't know where it came from, but it sure is yummy!" laughed Kinley.

Haylen and Wesson giggled.

The Tag-Alongs

Kinley quickly got ready for bed. Mommy came in and sang and said prayers with her. Daddy came in and tucked her unicorn quilt around her and kissed her cheek.

Kinley waited for them to leave so she could get ready for her next adventure. So, again, she said, "Good night, Mommy. Good night, Daddy. I love you."

"We love you too," they said.

Kinley closed her eyes and pretended to be asleep. Mommy and Daddy still didn't leave. "Why are you still here?" Kinley asked.

Daddy said, "Oh, we are going to hang out here for a while. Mommy and I want to know where the tadpoles, fireflies, gemstones . . . all the items that have turned up here in the last few mornings have come from."

Just then, Haylen and Wesson came into Kinley's room. Mommy and Daddy looked at each other with wonder in their eyes.

Wesson said, "Uh-oh, we will go back to our rooms."

"Um, no," Kinley said. "Mommy and Daddy want to know where we found the gemstones, walnuts, and the other things."

"Oh gosh," Wesson said.

Next thing you know, Grammy rushed into the room. "Sorry, I am late guys. Papa . . . Oh, hi!" she said to Mommy and Daddy.

"Mom," said Daddy, "what is going on here?"

"Well, we all know how Kinley doesn't like to go to bed, so we decided to go on adventures. After our first one, Wesson and Haylen wanted to go too."

"May we come on your adventure tonight?" asked Daddy.

"Sure!" everyone said.

So Kinley said,

"I will never leave you,

I will always take care of you,

And I will love you forever and ever . . .

No matter what."

"Ready! Let's load up, everyone," said Grammy.

It was a tight fit with Mommy and Daddy along. They got in the back of the UTV, and Daddy held Haylen. Up front, Kinley sat between Wesson and Grammy.

"Hold on," Grammy said, as she started the UTV and put it in gear.

Grammy drove through the backyard past the hummingbird feeder Mommy hung beneath the maple trees. They drove on the path until they got to the opening that led into the woods. But Grammy stopped.

"What's wrong?" Wesson asked.

"A hemlock tree has fallen across our trail."

"Come on, Wes," said Daddy, "we can move it out of the way."

They moved the tree off to the side well out of the way of the UTV. They got back in, and they continued down the steep hill, around a sharp curve, over a bridge, one more curve, and climbed up the muddy hill.

Mud splashed and Daddy said, "Hey, we're getting hit with mud back here."

"Yeah," said Wesson, "I got a glob of it on my face!"

Kinley said, "I didn't get hit with any mud."

"I could make it happen," laughed Mommy.

Down the path just a little more and Wesson said, "I see Dad's tree stand."

"Yes, you are right," said Daddy who was staring at the bottom of the tree.

There were the two little wood sprites, Bob and Bill.

Daddy said, "Hi, I'm Paul. Who are you?"

"I'm Bob," said the handsome wood sprite.

"Yes, I am Bill," said the little man with the red beard.

Haylen pointed to Daddy's beard and Bill's beard and said, "Pretty." Bill's face turned red, and Daddy cleared his throat.

Kinley said, "These are our friends, the wood sprites."

Mommy looked at the jars in the little men's hands. "So do you collect lightning bugs?" she asked.

"Yes," said Bob, "they light our way as we go through the woods at night."

"One mystery solved," said Mommy, "four to go."

Daddy chuckled.

Grammy said, "We'd better be on our way. We have to answer some questions Mommy and Daddy have."

They said goodbye to the little men, and Grammy started driving. In just a short time, they were at the blackberry patch.

"Do you think we will see Black Beary?" asked Kinley.

"I hope so," said Wes.

"Black Bee," said Haylen.

Grammy shut off the engine, and the children got out. "He might not come out. You know how shy he is," said Grammy.

Wesson called, "Black Beary!"

Kinley yelled, "Black Beary, it's us! We have our parents with us."

Haylen called, "Black Bee, come out, come out."

Grammy spotted a hemlock tree. She could see Black Beary hiding behind it. Finally, Black Beary looked around the tree. The children could see his round ear and pointed nose.

"It's okay," said Wesson. "You are safe."

"Yes, our parents are with us," said Haylen.

"Well, okay," Black Beary said, as he stepped out from behind the tree.

"Do you have enough honey?" asked Grammy.

"More than enough," said Black Beary. "Do you have enough blackberries?"

"Yes," said Grammy. "I can see we need to come out and pick some more."

"Mystery number two solved," said Mommy and Daddy together.

"Well, we have more visits to make, but we will come and see you soon," said Grammy.

"I will look forward to it," said Black Beary.

"Load up, everyone!" said Grammy. "We will go see Felicity Frog next. Would you like to drive, Daddy?"

"Okay," said Daddy. Mommy gave Daddy a funny look. He drove to Felicity's pond without needing any directions from Grammy.

Wesson said, "Hi, Felicity! How are you?"

Haylen said, "Frog?"

Kinley said, "We have something for you. Grammy, can you get it out?" Grammy reached into the back of the UTV and picked up a ten-gallon aquarium.

"Here, Mom, let me get that for you. It looks heavy," said Daddy. Daddy took the aquarium over to Felicity's pond.

Kinley said, "Here, all nine of them have successfully turned into frogs."

"Would you like me to put them in the grass?" asked Daddy.

"Yes, thank you," Felicity said. "And thanks again for digging this wonderful pond for my friends and me."

Haylen was counting the frogs, as Daddy put each one in the tall green grass. Mommy gave Daddy a sharp look. Daddy got a sheepish grin on his face and said, "I'll explain later."

"Mystery number three solved," said Wesson.

"Next," Kinley said, "we need to go to the Sparkling Gemstone Path."

"Got it!" Grammy said. She drove to the tunnel. Along they went, and Mommy enjoyed seeing all the gemstones on the walls of the tunnel. They traveled under the rainbow, and Ruby was there to greet them.

"Hello, again!" said Ruby.

"We brought our parents this time," said Wesson.

"I'm glad," said Ruby. "Remember, unicorns to the right, and kitchen to the left. And be sure to take your mom to the gemstone path to pick out her souvenir."

Wesson headed for the kitchen and Paul followed.

"What?" said Paul. "This trip has made me hungry too!"

Grammy, Mommy, and the girls went to ride unicorns. They went to the gemstone path where Mommy picked out a diamond.

When everyone got back together, Kinley said, "Guess what, Daddy! Mommy believes in unicorns too!"

Together, the children said, "Mystery number four solved, one more to go!"

Finally, the group came to the walnut trees. They got out of the UTV, and Daddy yelled, "Ouch, what was that?"

"Hey, Duncan, George, it is us," said Grammy.

"Whoopsie," said Duncan, "sorry about that."

"Where is that voice coming from?" asked Mommy.

"Up here," answered George.

"You pelted me with a walnut. It felt like a baseball!" exclaimed Daddy.

"How has the walnut gathering been going? Do you have enough for winter?" asked Grammy.

"Oh, yes, indeed. Now we are starting on acorns," said the two squirrels together.

"We'll help," said Grammy.

The group helped the little squirrels until they said they had enough walnuts.

"Well, we can head home now," said Grammy.

The children looked disappointed but tired.

Mommy said, "Mystery number five solved."

They headed along the path home. Kinley asked, "Now that you know about our adventures, do they have to end?"

"I think Mommy, Grammy, and I will have to talk about that," answered Daddy.

When they got home, everyone said goodbye to Grammy. Before she headed home, Grammy turned to Kinley and winked at her. Kinley smiled. They both knew the adventures were not going to end.

About the Book

Kinley doesn't like to go to bed. She doesn't want to waste time or miss something exciting.

Grammy and Kinley talk; Grammy understands completely. She doesn't like to go to bed either. So they agree at bedtime Kinley will say their special saying. After that, Grammy arrives in her shiny blue four-wheeler. Each night they go on a different adventure where they meet two wood sprites; a hungry black bear; a frog named Felicity; two squirrels, George and Duncan; and walk the Sparkling Gemstone Path.

Follow along as you read about their adventures that take place in the family's eighty-acre woods.

About the Author

Patti Pavolko is a wife, mother, grandmother, and retired special education teacher. She has been married to her best friend and hero, Dennis, for thirty-nine years. They have two children, Paul and Leslie; and three grandchildren—Wesson, Kinley, and Haylen.

She attended Edinboro State College from 1978–1982 where she pursued a double major. She graduated with a Bachelor of Science degree in Elementary and Special Education. She taught seventh-, eighth- and ninth-grade learning support at Conneaut Lake High School for one year. She then spent thirty-two years teaching learning support at Springfield Elementary School. She retired in 2015 and is now a stay-at-home grandmother. She enjoys riding her four-wheeler, picking blackberries, quilting, and playing with her grandchildren.

Printed in the United States
by Baker & Taylor Publisher Services